To Mstislav Rostropovitch and Jean-Sebastien Bach from which notes blow oftenly on my words.
Roxane

For my parents, Pierrot and Colombine, at seventeen years old.
Cathy

© Éditions Philippe Auzou, 2007
First published in France by éditions Auzou, 2007

HAMMOND World Atlas
Part of the Langenscheidt Publishing Group

Published in the United States and its territories by
HAMMOND WORLD ATLAS CORPORATION
Part of the Langenscheidt Publishing Group
36-36 33rd Street
Long Island City, NY 11106

Translator: Susan Allen Maurin

Printed and bound in China

ISBN-13: 978-0841-671386

Give Me the Moon

In Italian, English, and German,
a violoncello is called a "cello" . . .

Perhaps this story is the reason why . . .

A tale by Roxane Marie Galliez
Illustrated by Cathy Delanssay

Lulled by its lagoon, the city of Venice dreams and dances under scattered cotton petals of snow. Winter has arrived and the wind blows, but a crowd, huddled close together, gathers at Saint Mark's Square.

Marcello, a Venetian poet, plays his violin. Even the clouds pause to listen to him play.
With his head bowed over his instrument, he doesn't see how moved the young girls are, watching him.

He only sees the prettiest girl, Ava, in her cotton dress, deeply touched by his beautiful song. They don't speak to each other, and they don't need to. The violin sings of their new friendship.

But because of the words that go unsaid,

Ava has doubts about Marcello.

"Sometimes, I would like to be a violin,
to be held in his arms, and to feel his
cheek against mine.

But Marcello doesn't speak, he plays his violin.

He doesn't hear my words,
he only listens to his music.

And he doesn't pay any attention to me."

Kind Vincent heard Ava. He had secretly been in love with her for many years.

He went to her and promised her the world, in return for just one kiss.

"Nothing that you could offer me could ever be as beautiful as Marcello's music," she said to him.

"But Ava, he offers his music to everyone! All you have to do is ask, and I'll give you something that no one else could ever possess," he replied.

"Ask me for the moon, and I'll give it to you."

But she didn't want the moon. She wanted true love.
She wondered if it was Marcello she loved so much,
or only his music.

Ava continued to wonder about this, when, one night,
Vincent climbed up to her balcony and tapped on her
window. He was holding a long golden thread,
and tied to the end of it was the moon,
full and round.

"Vincent! How did you catch the moon ?" Ava asked.

"I just told the moon that I loved you, and it let me come near," he replied.

Vincent kissed Ava,

their hearts were beating . . .

And the moon carried the lovers away . . .

Ava no longer thought of Marcello,
but the musician had not forgotten her.

She was no longer there to listen to him, so he stopped playing.
The young girls walked away.
Handsome Marcello, who had always been a little proud,
didn't want anyone to know of his sadness.

So he wrapped his heart in a thick armor to protect
his feelings and keep himself from being hurt.

But at night, when no one could see him, he huddled up in his
garden and cried. He cried for Ava's absence, he cried for
the emptiness he felt, and he cried because he didn't understand
why the music no longer flowed through his fingers.

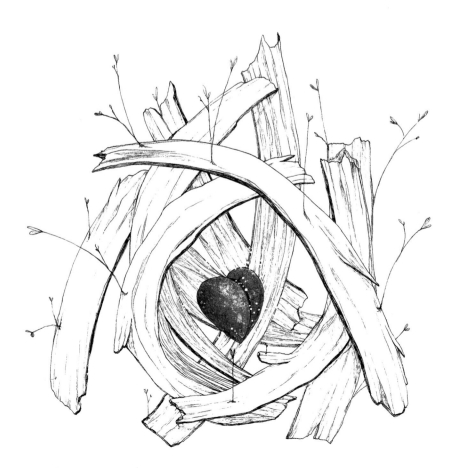

High up on the moon,
Ava caught sight of Marcello
and was moved by his sadness.

Two tears ran down her cheek,
bounced off the edge of the moon,
and, taking moon dust with them,
landed on the Earth.

One of the tears sank into the soft ground
and wrapped itself around a seed that had been
asleep for a very long time.

In just one day
and one night,
the seed sprouted and

grew…

And a big, brown tree shot up…

It was a special tree, with a wide, cavernous trunk.
Its leaves were shiny and silver, and it was strong and
impressive, while all the other trees were gnarled and bare.

The following night, Marcello was on his way to the garden when he noticed the new tree that had suddenly appeared.

At that very moment, the moon came out, and Marcello saw his beautiful Ava.

"Ava, please come back! I can't play my music without you . . . Ava!" he said.

But Ava was too far away and did not hear him.
For the first time since the young girl had left, Marcello picked up his violin and played. He played the sweetest notes, but Ava still couldn't hear . . .

"I need a bigger violin. An instrument that can carry my music to the moon, an instrument with a deep voice that will tell Ava that she is my muse and my friend."

Marcello looked at the big tree lit up by the night, and he decided to take it home with him.

He cut down the tree, sanded it, and polished it to make a new instrument. Then, he took his new instrument up to the highest balcony of his home, and began to play.

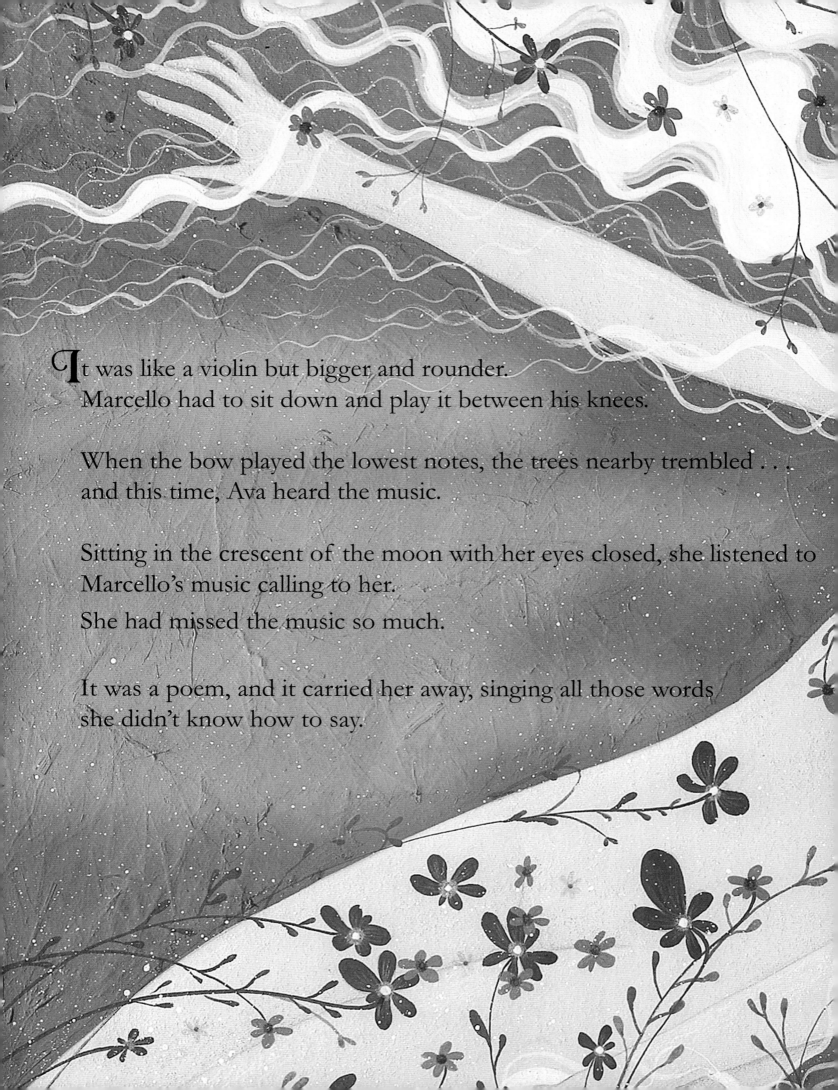

It was like a violin but bigger and rounder.
Marcello had to sit down and play it between his knees.

When the bow played the lowest notes, the trees nearby trembled . . .
and this time, Ava heard the music.

Sitting in the crescent of the moon with her eyes closed, she listened to
Marcello's music calling to her.
She had missed the music so much.

It was a poem, and it carried her away, singing all those words
she didn't know how to say.

Hearing the beautiful sound of Marcello's new instrument,
the Venetians opened their windows and their shutters, and
still half-asleep, they listened . . .

Some, guided by the far-off notes, got into their boats and
floated toward the music.

A strange crowd gathered underneath the balcony.
No one moved, no one spoke . . . everyone was captivated.

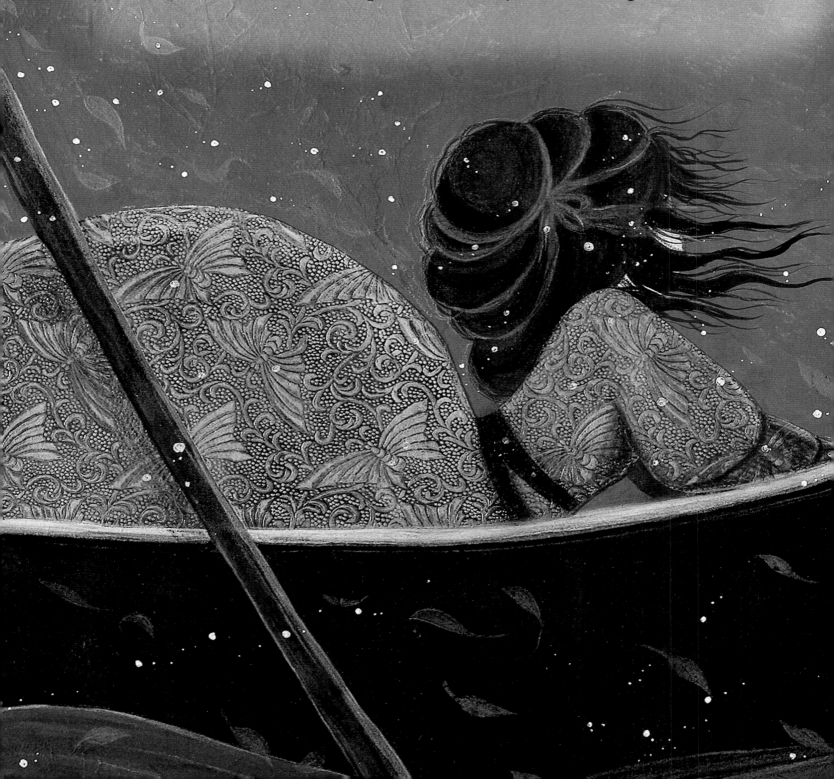

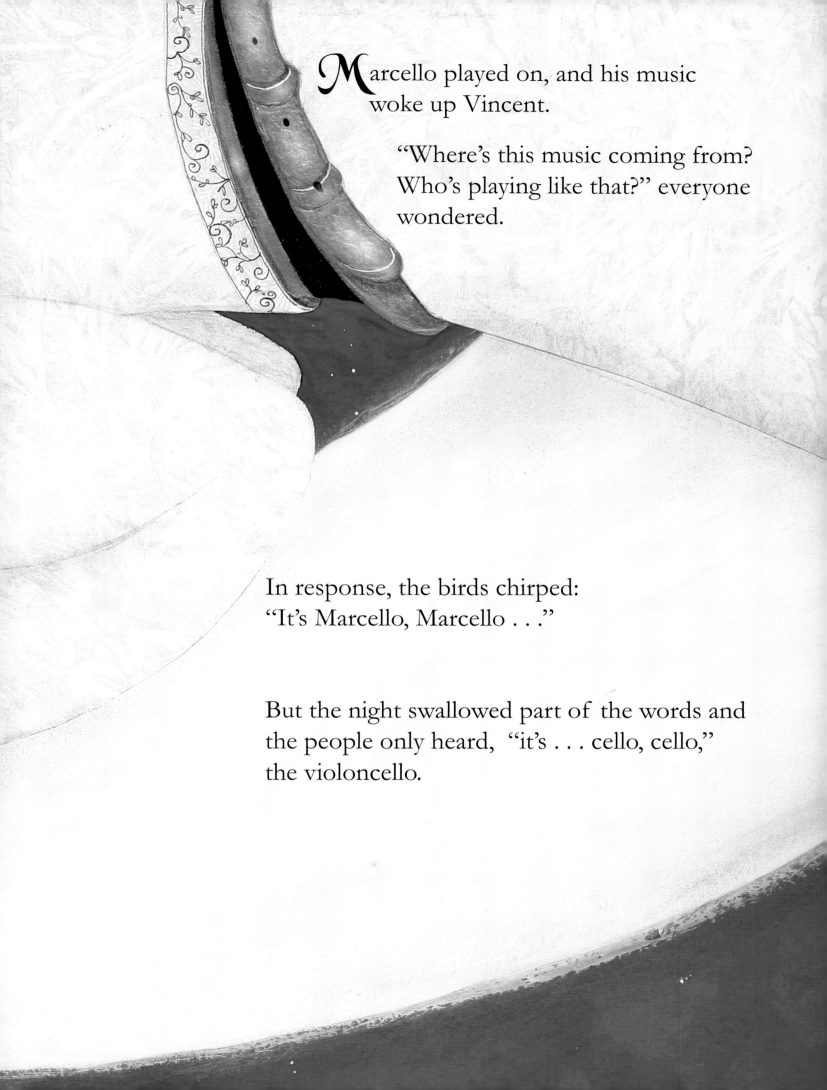

Marcello played on, and his music woke up Vincent.

"Where's this music coming from? Who's playing like that?" everyone wondered.

In response, the birds chirped: "It's Marcello, Marcello . . ."

But the night swallowed part of the words and the people only heard, "it's . . . cello, cello," the violoncello.

The music was so lovely that it brought peace to everyone who heard it . . .

But Vincent was nervous.

"Ava, my darling, if he's the one you love, then go to him, I'll understand. As soon as dawn breaks, you shall become a dove and fly to him," Vincent said.

"If you decide to stay, you will become a girl again before midnight, and you will stay on Earth forever.

But if you want to come back, I will wait for you."

Dawn broke, and Marcello was still playing.

A dove landed on the tip of his instrument.
He did not look at it, but he knew it was there, and it
inspired him to play notes that were even more beautiful.

Marcello continued to play all day, discovering this new instrument that revealed his thoughts and feelings so well, an instrument with a voice so similar to his own, but capable of expressing emotions that no other sound could ever express.

Evening came, and still the dove didn't move.

Marcello felt alive again thanks to his new instrument.
It was true that Ava inspired him to play beautifully, and he loved her dearly . . . but he wasn't in love with her.

He didn't love her in the way that makes you lose yourself, as though in a dream.

A note touched Ava in a secret place, a place that she had
forgotten. It was low and soft, and it felt like a kiss.
She trembled, and then she understood.
It was the music she needed, not Marcello, even though she
was very fond of him.

When the note echoed inside her, she heard Vincent's voice whispering "I love you," again and again.

Marcello stopped playing, placed the cello on his knees, and, stroking the dove, said, "thank you."

They understood that, from now on, their lives would lead them in separate directions, and they parted.

Ava watched the moon slowly rising, and, with a flap of her wings, she flew back to Vincent, her true love.

Marcello continues to play for Ava, for Vincent, and for all those who need music in their life.

I am one of those who need music. The beauty of the cello touched me deep down and told me this story, which found a secret place in me, a forgotten place that has come to life again.

Listen close, and let yourself be carried away by the power of these deep strings, this warm wood. Let the notes enter . . .

They know the hidden pathways and will whisper stories to you and even secrets, perhaps.